Ugly Shy girl

Laura Dockrill

HARPER

Harper
An imprint of HarperCollins*Publishers*
77–85 Fulham Palace Road,
Hammersmith, London W6 8JB

www.harpercollins.co.uk

This paperback edition 2009
1

Copyright © Laura Dockrill 2009

Laura Dockrill asserts the moral right to
be identified as the author of this work

A catalogue record for this book is
available from the British Library

ISBN: 978 0 00 730128 7

Set in Carniola

Printed and bound in Great Britain by
Clays Ltd, St Ives plc

This book is for . . .

Ugly Shy girl

You might have once known somebody
like Ugly shy girl.

You might have even been like
her yourself.

SUNDAY.

Dear diary,

Today I went to the funfair with James. Mum made me go with him because she had a bum, legs and thigh class at the gym and felt guilty about leaving me indoors. James was an idiot the whole time.

I HATE HIM sometimes.

Especially today. On the way there he walked like ten paces infront of me and left me out of everything and when we got inside he

walked off with his stupid friends, they all went on the bumper cars and so I followed them. They all got in their own cars and left me to get in a car by myself. Then they proceeded to smash the shit out of me for like a million years, I ended up crashed in the corner, even the woman from the little booth had to come out and tell them to 'calm down'. The belt from the dodgems rubbed my neck and came out in a massive bruise. James said it looked like I had a lovebite. It does look like a lovebite! It's horrible, it looks purple and I just know I'm going to get teased about that tomorrow. Straight after that we went over to the waltzers, and when I went over to sit with them - (Alex and Tom, James says that Tom gets beaten up by his dad but you would never tell.

6

James told me "not to say anything" as if I
was desperate to catch a quiet moment with
Tom to go "Hi Tom, James told me you get
knocked about by your dad..." I hate that.
When people say "Don't say anything." It's like...
give me some bloody credit.)
Anyway... they shut the bar down really
quickly so I couldn't sit with them because
they are a bunch of dicks. So I had to
sit by myself because I was too shy to
ask for my money back.

I felt crap the whole time and the men
just kept spinning me round more and more,
because I was by myself I span faster than
everyone else. When it came to getting off
time I stood up and my dress had tore and
all I remember seeing was shreds of it left
on the seat. My knickers were showing. The
men laughed. Alex and Tom laughed too, James
pretended not to know me. I had to
phone dad from a phone box to come and
get me. He tried to cheer me up by playing
David Bowie in the car... but... it didn't
work. I was too embarrassed. Even as I'm
writing this now I feel sick and embarrassed,
I have to keep closing my eyes to forget it.
Sometimes I push my fingers into my eyes until
it hurts, so I forget embarrassing stuff. I
push and don't stop pushing until I see hundreds of
white circles.

Once I pushed my eyes in so hard that when I

7

Woke up the next morning I made myself think I had glass trapped in my eyes and dad took me to the optician and the optician said that I had been pushing my eyes way too hard and asked me why I did it... and I said...

"To forget." and my dad said, "That's what alcohol's for love." Trying to be funny. It wasn't, it was annoying.

She gave me some drops but I've lost them now.

Night
X Abigail.

The story I am about to unravel starts in a normal place, like I don't know, Streatham or Elm Park . . . except not in London because there are more trees...

A normal place where people know each other a little bit more and

* Still go to church on a Sunday
* And bake cakes to raise money for the church
* Where tea time is at 5.30
* And shops shut at 6.
* And young people do not curse or say, 'I want.'
* And people still buy After Eights and buy loaves that come in brown paper bags and fight for rashers of bacon.
* And sometimes share the same bath water . . .

A place where the kids sit and smoke in bus shelters and steal traffic cones and write 'EMMA 4 BEN 4 EVA' on the sides of bridges, that kind of place. On a normal road with a couple of paper shops, a post office, a few pigeons squabbling over a small discarded leg of fried chicken; is a normal brick house and inside live a very out of the ordinary family indeed.

The reason the Rodgers are so out of the ordinary is because they don't really behave like a family at all. They are almost like a bunch of lodgers living in separate rooms, never crossing paths, sneakily stealing a blob of

Some monk
I'm unsure
whe
the
a
t

James'
room

Attic...

The parents room.

Abigails
room

Bathroom...

The sitting room...

ZZZpizzaz

The kitchen...

supposed to be stairs...
erm... use your imagination.

10

butter or a drop of milk. It wasn't always like this, they *had* tried once upon a time, but now they were like a reject puzzle from the puzzle factory. No matter how hard they tried the pieces didn't fit, the components not compatible.

This is Mrs Rodgers . . . or Camilla. Notice the tadpole like eyebrows, the heavy pencil that colours them in and the lipstick. She has worn that shade her entire lipstick-wearing life, '*Flawless*'. The manufacturers went bust in the late nineteen so she buys it in bulk online. Camilla is a time-bomb waiting to go off, filling up her day with *vital* time-saving activities such as making her breakfast the night before work or using disposable plates and cutlery. Mrs Rodgers is obsessed with anything 'handy'; pocket-sized 6pk tissues, and disinfectant hand spray, diaries that come with a pen. Camilla believes strictly in routine and order, she has trained her body like a scientist would a robot, disciplining herself not to eat, sleep or even use the toilet unless absolutely necessary. She never burps or coughs, sneezes or yawns. She is like a mechanical doll. Mrs Rodgers met Mr Rodgers in the days when she was young and busty; both were two odd strays at a charity summer fête and had no choice but to join forces in a 3-legged race. They came last and laughed about it at the time but Mrs Rodgers has never forgiven Colin for allowing them to come last and probably never will . . . actually . . . this is my story . . . no, she will never forgive him.

Colin, (Mr Rodgers), was always a happy child. Growing up he was known for his kindness to animals and was encouraged to study biology at school to further his interest. Sadly, he suffered from dyslexia and without the support, failed his exams. Two days after his devastating results, Colin's father was hit by a tractor and with two younger sisters and a widowed mother, Colin, being the devoted brother and son he was, saw no other choice than to take over his father's job as a farmer. However, he was kicked in the face by his favourite horse Bracken (by accident) which not only meant he suffered from a slight case of brain damage, he also managed to lose every tooth in his pie hole. Nice. Colin decided not to have his teeth replaced. He firmly believes that everything happens for a reason. These days, Colin likes nothing more than the sofa and watching recorded videotapes of snooker. He survives on the happiness in his gut that reminds him his cup is always half full. As much as he enjoys his nightcap, 'cheese on toast with a beer mixed in' (I'm terribly sorry, I don't know what that's called), there is nothing that makes him drunker than life itself. Colin just has a beautiful soul and although his life hasn't panned out exactly as he'd planned, he wouldn't change a single bit of it.

James is their twenty-year-old son. He likes these three things; cars, talking about his 21st birthday and a girl called Rebecca Great who has a slight case of nappy rash around the lower half of her neck. To his face, Rebecca likes to pretend she fancies James, but really, behind his back, she says some wretched things, aimed mainly at the spare tooth that pokes out of his gum that she refers to as 'the tusk'.

And then there lives one other person. A person that is more private and quiet than all of those we've just encountered. Abigail is so shy it's a wonder how people ever see her. For she is like a tiny speck of dust that the Hoover has forgotten to suck up. Unlike most seventeen year olds, Abigail has a very difficult life, she is plagued with constant cruelty and downright meanness. There is always somebody at college giving her a hard time and she is bullied, horrendously. The Rodgers have no idea that their daughter is so terribly unpopular . . . or that she is known as the Ugly Shy Girl.

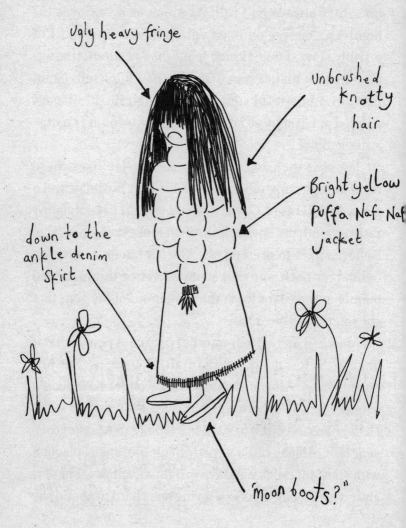

ugly heavy fringe

unbrushed knotty hair

Bright yellow Puffa Naf-Naf jacket

down to the ankle denim skirt

'moon boots?"

14

Dear diary.

Go back to college tomorrow. Mum left new stationary on my bed. I finally got a flip rulers. It's about 10 years too late but anyway. I've done no work, I can't be bothered... James keeps ringing Rebecca, I hear him all the time on his stupid little retard mobile saying ridiculous crap like "Text me later" and then sometimes getting confident and adding shit like "babe" on the end which makes me want to be sick in his face. She's 17 - 11 what is he thinking? He's such a pervert and more importantly Rebecca Great is not a nice person. She is a bitch with an ironic Sur-name. FULL STOP! If she gives me crap tomorrow I will say something really clever and harsh about her!! Infront of everyone and make her look like a TWAT... I will have to think of something later.

I've decided that Will Smith ~~might~~ might have to be my favourite celebrity. It used to be Peter Crouch.

I've put on weight, I don't know how much because I don't weigh myself... but my clothes feel a bit tight. I don't ever remember putting on weight before, my aunty used to always talk about it, you know, about christmas ~~and the~~ the pounds and it never happened to me. This year Pilling though, I can feel it. I like chocolate too much that's why. But I'm never not going to eat it. It's probably my favourite thing...

I found some exfoliator in the bathroom cupboard. I wanted to put it on my face but the first warning was - DO NOT USE ON FACE, which is really annoying to be honest. I put it on my arms and bum. I've got spots on my bum. I guess that's why it kind of works for me that I don't like to wear explicit, showy affy clothes... like Florence or Leilah. Sometimes they come into college dressed like the pussycat dolls... so sluts basically. The boys pretend they like it, but really, if I was a boy I wouldn't want to go out with a girl that dressed like that. leaves nothing to the imagination. Not that a boy would want his girlfriend to dress like ~~me~~ me, but I'm sure the two styles could meet in the middle? maybe I could knock up some designs? I wonder if you have to be able to draw to be a fashion designer?

MOM finally spoke to dad this evening. He was asleep on the sofa when she got back from work. She picked up his dirty socks, rolled them into a ball, threw them at his head and then she leaned right into his face and said, "Do you enjoy being so bloody useless?"

She can be a real cow sometimes. Even though Dad is a bit useless, that's not the point. It's unfair of her to be so cruel to him - he's harmless.

I'm dreading ~~still~~ tomorrow but I'm hoping that some people might have made "be nicer to Abigail" their new year resolution. Although saying that... I'm the sort of person that people give up resolutions for. I'm the reason some people go to college ~~am~~ aren't I?

Night. x
Abigail.

Abigail walked up to her college entrance to find Matt sitting on the wall waiting for her.

'Hey buddy, you're five minutes early . . . fresh start to the New Year, eh?' he laughed. Colleges have these people, support assistants, agony aunts, whatever you like to dress it up as and they are assigned to a case, like a detective, to shadow. To make sure that their days run smoothly. At this college they are known as 'buddies' and Matt is Abigail's *buddy*. Some people would say that Abigail was lucky that her buddy wasn't a tight-fisted old hag with a melting face but Matt was just as difficult to get along with for different reasons. Matt was 32 years old. When his head wasn't consumed by a tight beanie, he had his hair all spiked up like he had used a whole tub of Brylcreem . . . (excuse me . . . I mean . . . Wella) to get that *out of bed look.* He played around with it all the time, constantly referring to it as his *flea pit* but the warm smells of coconut shampoo and limey gel haunted him on his day to day whereabouts; it was very clear that his hair was washed more than the hands of the man with OCD. Matt wore baggy jeans that cut an inch or two too high around the leg; sort of swung around his ankles, showing off his Family Guy socks, making him look very awkward and slightly try-hard. Then there was that skater chain that hung so blatantly from his side pocket, reflecting Abigail's dismal grimace and every other spare reflection in its

twinkling presence, screaming, 'I'M MASSIVLY OVER-
PRICED, WAS I EVEN BOUGHT FROM A COOL
SHOP? WHAT THE HELL AM I USED FOR?' Matt had
the vocabulary of a fourteen year old; he used words like
'sick', 'wicked' and his good old favourite, 'random'.

'It's raining, *random.*'

'Hey, the guys have got a football, we should totally
play, could be *random*?'

Which frustrated Abigail because she found that
when something was actually 'random' she couldn't bring
herself to use the word
itself, she was tired of
having to find alternatives
. . . 'Yes, the lottery balls
are chosen at . . . melon?
Transformer? Broomstick?'
You see, it just doesn't
work.

This wasn't the only
thing that annoyed
Abigail, it was the relentless
refusal to give-up on her. He
loved it. Abigail spent almost
everyday giving off all the
signals that she didn't need
him around. When he

spoke – she stared at the floor, folding her arms aggressively, scuffing her boots along the walls. When he sat near her at lunch – she would get up and move away but he would still come after her, like the stinky boy in class with the bad breath and the dried smudges of sleep sculpted around his eyes. He would still want to be next to her to make more pointless comments about the weather or The Simpsons or what he had eaten for breakfast. 'Toast. Random.' The 'buddy' system was even more painful as it quite frankly made matters worse. Bullies just made jokes about Abigail going out with a teacher, the girls would crack up laughing for no reason at all whenever the two of them walked past and the boys would make ludicrous sex noises:

'FUCK ME, MATT.'

'ONLY WITH A BLINDFOLD YOU UGLY SHY BITCH.'

Matt was *so* polite and *so* protective of Abigail he would just play along with the comments, laughing hysterically, creasing his newly wrinkled face and sometimes overacting by putting a hand on his stomach. 'You guys!' he'd hoot breathlessly, dramatically slapping his thigh. Matt wasn't fooling anybody; he was as transparent as a looking-glass. Abigail knew that she had no friends; she knew that she was the pinnacle of everybody's fun and she knew that it was her that everybody was laughing at. She *just* knew.

So when Matt greeted her at the entrance to college at the start of the new term, she already had a pretty decent idea of what the next few months were going to work out like. (Which is why she pretended not to notice him.)

Dear diary

I'm in the library. Miss Greg didn't come in today. Mr Howell did come in to explain that she had the flu, but she is obviously having a mental breakdown. She can't even hold the board pen straight. Everyone in the class are real idiots to her, so I'm not suprised she's having a mental breakdown. Somebody should send her some flowers... anyway... that's why we're in the library for a double period.

I'm SO bloody sick of Matt. I know he's trying to be nice...if I hear that again I'll kill myself. I KNOW he's only trying to be nice but he's so annoying. And it's not that I want to be cool, I couldn't give the two shits about looking cool, and I think we're passed that stage now. But it's like he pulls the sleeve of my coat and he goes "I love your coat chick it's so retro." First of all he's seen my coat a million times now, I wear the crusty thing everyday and second of all - IT'S CRAP... I know it's a pile of crap. I don't need his retro bollocks, I don't need his patronising comments.

22

I should get a new coat I spose. Mum and dad
have both offered to get me a new one but
I know I will just pick something that looks
the same as this one and that would be
even worse... a _new_ puffa jacket... now thats
just taking the piss, at least with this one
people dont ask questions - they just assume I'm
really poor - which is better than having bad style...
I think... Is it? Especially now that I'm considering
pursuing a career in fashion.

  Bianca and Jessica are whispering about
Yasmin. They're saying she has B.O.
  Cows.

Matt was engulfed in some meaningful conversation about Japan with the librarian. Rebecca, Florence and Leilah paraded in through the library doors like three long-legged exotic birds and began gabbling over the other side of the room,

'Just a minute, Matt,' the librarian excused herself. 'Girls, you know the library policy, keep it down, please. Thank you.' To which Rebecca stuck up her middle finger as proud as a kitten that had managed to shit on the expensive rug. Then the whispering began. Rebecca was more of a threat to Abigail in comparison to everybody else, the reason being, she was the only person from the college that had been to her house. She came over to 'knock for James' and ended up having a glass of lemonade and a cherry bakewell. This meant that Rebecca knew perhaps an extra 60% more information about Abigail a.k.a Ugly Shy Girl than the rest of the outside world, which made Abigail feel slightly vulnerable and certainly uneasy. Rebecca was also renowned for being a top-class bitch. She had mastered the art of being a bully. Now, whispering across the room she had Florence and Leilah suckling on her words like bees on nectar. And her strong eyes, as fierce as two axes, were pinned to Abigail, strangling her with their pupils. Florence got up and sauntered over to Abigail, pulling up the chair opposite her and swinging it round so she was sitting on it back to front. Just like that song sung by that woman with lots of hair, this was irony in its finest form. Abigail was caught like a fly under a swot. The girls had slipped in through the cracks in the brickwork and where was Matt? Having a blast with the Librarian in the turtleneck.

'Rebecca and Leilah reckon you haven't got any pubes. I'm saying you do. You do right? If you do could you pull out a few so I can show them to shut them up?' snickered Florence. Abigail picked at the edges of her diary.

'Well you have or you haven't?' Florence started again.

Abigail's head was facing so far forward it felt as though it could snap. Her fringe smothered her eyes which were scampering wildly about, searching for an escape.

'Or are you one of those girls that are dark on top but ginger downstairs. Hope not. You can felt tip them, you know. Not with a Berol though, it has to be a permanent marker really.'

Abigail's heart was beating so quickly she was sure everyone could hear it. Leilah and Rebecca sat across the room, bog-eyed and long-necked.

There was a long, painful silence.

'Agh, who cares anyway? She's a baby, she hasn't got any.' Rebecca chuckled wickedly, threw her head back and snatched a copy of HEAT magazine off Leilah, flicking through it without glancing at a single page. Then her face contorted into a grimace and she began to waft her hand dramatically in front of her face.

'Saying that though, she certainly doesn't smell like a baby. Ugh, she smells like rotten fish. Shut your legs can you, Ugly Shy Girl? Jesus, I can smell you from here.'

Rebecca carried on wafting the nonexistent stench out of her face.

'I can't smell anything,' said a confused Leilah.

'Me neither,' huffed Florence, annoyed. Both girls were clearly not horrid enough to catch onto Rebecca's vile rope.

'Well you're lucky, it's disgusting,' Rebecca said, peering back down at her magazine. 'I'm bored of this, let's go and watch Amy Benton in her leotard, she's got stretch marks up to her eye balls.'

Abigail, who had been rooted to the spot, paralysed by fear, breathed a sigh of relief as Matt plodded into the room, grinning like a happy bear. 'The librarian is from Japan. I so totally went there for a year. Random.'

'Another day with no trouble then. See, it works, doesn't it? Having your buddy with you during the day?' Matt said, shuffling his papers scrawled with colour co-ordinated notes and little scribbles of rocket ships and monsters with long teeth. Ugly Shy Girl, I mean Abigail, shrugged and looked about the room, focusing on the damp patches in the corners, the second-hand filing cabinets with the bent sides, and the rust around the runners.

'Have you ever listened to Led Zeppelin?'

There was a knock at the door.

It was Rebecca.

'Hi, sir. You all right, Abigail? I was just wondering if I could get five minutes with you after you're finished with Abigail?' She dipped her eyes so they suddenly went all doe-like. She had applied a fresh layer of gloss to her lips. Abigail noticed how strange her name sounded coming out of Rebecca's mouth. She was so used to hearing the oh so familiar, 'Ugly Shy Girl.'

'Yes, of course, we'll be done pretty soon if you just want to hang about outside.'

'Yeah, sure.' Rebecca grinned, as nice as pie, the un-melted butter perched on her malicious tongue. The door closed again.

'Yeah sorry, where was I? Led Zeppelin? I'll make you a CD, I'll put some other stuff on there too, how about that?' Matt said, winding his headphones around his iPod. 'Sound all right?'

Ugly Shy Girl nodded. She rarely spoke to Matt, but she wasn't stupid, she knew when somebody was actually doing something kind for her.

'I'd like that,' she mumbled.

'Have a nice evening,' he said and opened the door for her. 'See you tomorrow for another *crazy* day, eh?' He saluted to her and signalled a 'chin-up'. Rebecca took no notice of Abigail as she passed by, she was busy texting on her phone. But before Abigail was out of earshot, she hissed, 'Whore' and stood up on her ostrich legs, moles scattered over them like bits of chocolate chip. She scooped her long dark hair over her shoulder, swanned into Matt's office and the door clicked shut behind her.

Abigail's walks home were never lonely, there was always somebody behind her calling her a 'tit' or a 'moose', asking her why she looked like she was going to the alps, or why she couldn't afford a hair cut. Today was one of the trickier days. The boys were at the bus stop and she knew them all from making her life difficult at secondary school. These were the boys who chose not to go to college but preferred to sit on the wall outside Tesco's smoking Sovereigns and drinking White Lightning.

'Oi, Ugly Shy Girl!' One of them tried to get her attention. It was Gary; he had once sat opposite Abigail at their previous school. Abigail recalled a particular art lesson where the task was to draw your reflection. Everybody sat around the room with their mirrors, the violin music playing in the background, shading their complexions, trying to capture their acne, the shape of their eyes. When it came to sharing their work at the end of the session, Gary had just drawn 'up Abigail's legs'. It wasn't even a good drawing; it was just a very badly drawn cartoon. The class loved it, they smacked the table with their fists, stomped their feet and began asking Gary if they could keep it. Abigail was humiliated; she'd had no idea that the mirror was even under the table. Her drawing was put on display, not because it was good, but because the teacher felt guilty; she too knew how it felt to be isolated from class, like being the only sober one at a riotous party, she identified with Abigail.

'HEL-LO! You got shit in your ears or what?' yelled Aran who was always known as being 'half a slice short of a sandwich'. He had once tried to shave three lines into his eyebrow and ended up cutting his forehead and removing his eyelashes. Aran had short-back-and-sides with peroxide tips that had gone a sort of chicken-korma greenish; he liked to go swimming and the chlorine had reacted with the bleach. Aran also had about five brown teeth that sat rooted at the bottom of his mouth like a rack of burnt sweetcorn. It would send shivers up anyone's spine to look at his putrid mouth. The other boys were clones of each other, lined up in their Diadora tracksuits, Reebok Classic trainers, and yellow gold rings.

Abigail pretended not to hear them; she was actually really good at that. It was amazing how helpful a fringe can be when it comes to avoiding sounds or people.

Then she heard the scramble for bikes and knew it was about time to pick up pace. She walked slightly faster but could hear the rumble of tyres behind her and had no choice but to run.

'GET HER!' roared one of the boys, and so they came, like a swarm of vicious hornets, she felt them behind her. Her heart began to rush and her skin prickled against the frosty air. Abigail was clumsy at the best of times and her down-to-the-ankles denim skirt, her heavy school bag and her long fringe only made her clumsier. She ran, ran as fast as she could, feeling vomit collecting in her throat, and her eyes burning against the sharp wind. The boys had found bin lids now and those who were better at riding were slamming them together with their hands, charging towards her in an angry parade. Just when she reached the familiar kerb that told her brain she was close to home she began to run faster, pounding round the corner, tears streaming down her hot face. The boys went straight past her and rode off laughing throwing the bin lids onto the pavement, smacking hands and spitting, their hearts all racing as one.

Abigail kept on running, her bag dangling half way down her body now and giving her ankle a good bruising. She threw herself into the house and went straight to her room where she shut the door and slammed her body onto her bed – which she knew was dramatic, but that's how she felt.

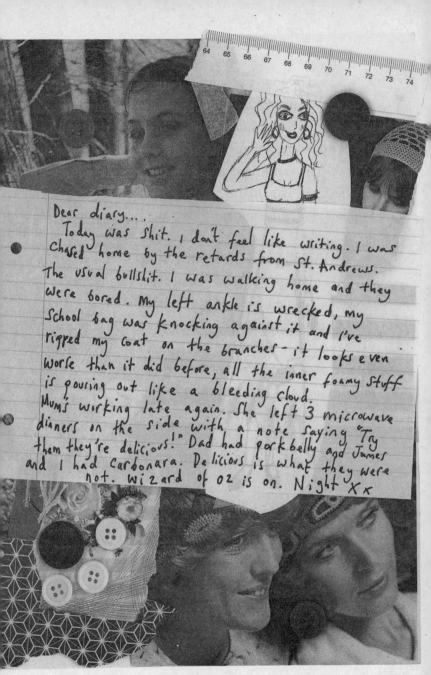

Dear diary....

Today was shit. I don't feel like writing. I was chased home by the retards from St. Andrews. The usual bullshit. I was walking home and they were bored. My left ankle is wrecked, my school bag was knocking against it and I've ripped my coat on the branches - it looks even worse than it did before, all the inner foamy stuff is pouring out like a bleeding cloud. Mum's working late again. She left 3 microwave dinners on the side with a note saying "Try them they're delicious!" Dad had pork belly and James and I had Carbonara. Delicious is what they were not. Wizard of oz is on. Night xx

Abigail woke up to the sound of drilling. She sat up and checked the time, 4.05 am. She wasn't childish but noises in the night *did* frighten her. It was one of those horrible moments when you feel too scared to sit in bed but too scared to go and investigate. She lay there for a bit, her eyes jerking about in their sockets, searching for light, her pupils as wide as saucers. Then she heard James' door open.

'WHAT THE HELL IS GOING ON?' he yelled, his voice far more grizzly than usual. The drilling didn't stop. Abigail got up and opened her door too.

'I'm gonna go and see,' James grunted at her. His hair was greasy and matted, he smelt the same way your hand smells after holding a copper coin for ages, hot, metallic and dirty. Abigail followed him.

In the living room, dressed in her work suit still looking as fresh and uncreased at it did that morning, her hair firmly in place, was their mother drilling holes into the wall.

'MUM! MUM!' James shouted and she swung round, switching off the drill as she did so

'What are you doing up?' she asked in a surprised tone.

'You're drilling at four in the morning, are you some sort of crazy person? What is going on? I've got stuff to do tomorrow,' he said, his voice high-pitched and whiney.

'Well, if your father wasn't so incredibly talented at being such a LAZY GOOD FOR NOTHING PIG, I wouldn't have to be putting my own shelves up.' She eye-balled the ceiling.

'I don't believe this, this is beyond ridiculous, go to bed.' James tried to prise the drill from his mother but she held onto it. Abigail zoned out by drawing around the designs on the sofa with her fingertip, wondering why she had bothered to come downstairs in the first place.

'Go to bed? Darling, I'm not tired.' She tutted as if offended.

'Yes. You. Are.' James smiled wearily.

'No, I'm bloody not!' she muttered but dropped the drill to the floor, sighed and ushered them up the stairs. 'Night night, kids,' she whispered, before opening the door to her bedroom where Mr Rodgers was snoring away as happy as an elephant getting rid of an itch with a big stick.

'Just so you know,' she began, slamming on the lights and shaking Colin's shoulders forcefully which resulted only in a soft grumble, 'the kids HATE you for not putting those shelves up, I hope you feel terrible. I'm going to make some coffee,' and with that she flounced out of the room without switching off the lights. Abigail and James could hear her loud footsteps clanking back down the stairs and seconds later the drill was on once more.

'You're taking the piss now,' James howled as he bounded down the stairs again

'I'm taking the piss? *I'm the taking the piss?*' Her hands were flying round hysterically as though she were trying to catch some bats. 'I'm not Billy No Brains up there snoring my head off. One of these days I'll drill his arse to the wall. That'll wake the slob up. Fat, lazy, good for nothing SLOB.' The defeated James made his way back to his room and closed the door. Mrs Rodgers, teeth gritted, continued to drill until the neighbours knocked half an hour later to ask if everything was okay.

The next day, Abigail was feeling even more ropey than usual. She sat at the back of every class. She sometimes did not even bother to get her books out. She was one of those students with a star next to her name that meant, in one way or another, *Let this student get away with everything,*

i.e. not participating is class, chewing gum, sleeping, eating,
moisturising their kneecaps or elbows etc as they are being
bullied. Quite badly. Ta. Which she was aware of but never
really took advantage of, instead she saved them all up, for
days like this when she could just slump into the corner and
stare out of the window, wishing that the alarm would go off
for the fire drill.

Suddenly, two furrowed brows popped up at the little
classroom-door window. The door opened. It was the
receptionist.

'Hello, Nick. Sorry to interrupt your class but could I
steal Abigail for a short mo?' Abigail was resentful to 'be
stolen' but happy to get out of creating a 'group Bayeux
tapestry' even if only by the receptionist for just 'a short
mo'. Snaking down the corridor behind her, Abigail began
to think about why she might have been called out. She
couldn't bear it if she had been falsely blamed again for
graffiti, or the fag butts in the toilets.

'Sit down, Abigail. It's nothing to worry about, just a
couple of questions . . . Would you like some water?' the
receptionist asked. She had spinach in her teeth.

Abigail could have done with a drop but shook her
head. In came Mr Stanton.

'Hi there . . . err . . . sorry your name seems to have
escaped me . . . ' Mr Stanton began; obviously unaware that
Abigail was not the type to help people out in conversation.

'I . . . err . . . need to ask you a few questions about your buddy, Mr Matthew Gates.'

Abigail looked down at the floor. 'I believe you have a good relationship with him?' Abigail was mute.

'I'm sorry to be so direct, it's just that we need to get this sorted as soon as possible. Has Matthew, ever tried to . . .

how shall I put it? *Caress* you?' Mr Stanton put the question to Abigail, who sat stiffly on the chair and then shook her head.

'No? Never *touched* you in a private way?' Mr Stanton attempted again. '*Inappropriately?*'

Abigail shook her head.

'Never asked, perhaps, if *you* would, I don't know, *touch* him, has he ever asked a personal *favour* from you?' Mr Stanton's eyes looked like two cannons, intense behind his spectacles. Abigail shook her head again and realising the gravity of the conversation said, 'No. Never. He's my buddy.'

'Thank you then . . . errr . . . if you do think of anything, please let us know.' Because people do seem to forget those things don't they? Really. As if.

As she made her way back to the classroom, she saw Mr Stanton going back into his office where Rebecca sat with the college nurse and a box of tissues crying her eyes out. Abigail, for one moment, was in two minds.

The rest of the day without Matt was a struggle. The canteen was like a circus. It was over crowded and claus-trophobic and smelt like oil and crayon. Posters on the wood-chip wall reminded Abigail just how cruddy it actu-ally was:–

'*GOOD FOOD CAN BE TASTY*' '*AN APPLE A DAY KEEPS THE DOCTOR AWAY*' '*A BALANCED DIET IS A*

GOOD DIET.' The canteen supervisor obviously found it irrelevant that each poster was drenched in grease.

There is something strange about the whole make up of a college. It sort of floats in this non-existent, implacable area; it's the purgatory of education. Kids with any brains would stick to the sixth form of their secondary school; at least then you wouldn't have the hassle of making and keeping a new set of friends for two years. The canteen though, this is where everything goes wrong. Its main function is supposed to be for students to re-fuel, to eat, to drink, to relax, to perhaps socialise? It's not there for table ownership, to say the fat people sit on that table and the thin people sit on this table, to pluck your eyebrows, to cut out your split ends, to make a comic book of 'How Alison and Sita were found lezzin' off in the changing room Part 3',

HOW ALISON AND SITA WERE FOUND LEZZIN' OFF IN THE CHANGING ROOM... PART III...

BY PENNY.

to pour a carton of juice into somebody's bag, to get off on making somebody's day a misery. College is for teenagers that have reached that weird age, like when you're twelve and you no longer want to wear the George from ASDA range of jumpers, but you can't fit into Warehouse or Oasis, and nor will your mother spend £40 for you to have a pair of jeans that you're just going to grow out of in six months. Being sixteen and seventeen is like that all over again. A bunch of wiggly, uneven misfits with hormones bouncing off the ceiling, caring far more what CD spins about inside their Discman than whether or not they're going to pass their A-Levels.

'Been dumped have you, skank?'

'Where's your man now, ho?'

'You all lonely now, Ugly Shy Girl? Boo hoo hoo . . .' Having been greeted by such delightful comments, Abigail had decided to eat her lunch sitting on the outside wall. These days she often made sandwiches to avoid eating in the canteen. Marcus Brigg was always outside at lunchtime. Today he had chewed an ink cartridge and blue ink trickled down his chin and in various designs on his hands and shoes. Another girl sat outside too, she was drawing the back of the school on a sketchpad. Abigail had never seen anybody dressed like her before. She was clothed entirely in black with lots of silver necklaces, her lips smothered in black lipstick. Abigail didn't even know you could get black lipstick. Abigail stared at her intensely. She felt addicted to this girl's face. Who was she? Where did she come from?

Abigail could hear mopeds whizzing by on the nearby road. She knew it was the boys from her year, they always left at lunchtime and came back with chip rolls. She heard the bikes park up and the boys began talking and laughing. Two walked in, one still had his helmet on and the other was slightly shorter with tiny cornrows.

'How long tho' does it take for a whole building tho'? To like burn down?' one asked the other.

'What? As in shit, boy, that building is getting licked? Or just say like a house fire?'

'Nah, I'm talking 'bout *flames,* boy.'

'Pshhhh . . . hours . . . days . . . maybe?'

'Would be kinda sick tho', watching it would be kinda mad, like, imagine dat, if in science we could just sit dere an burn shit. I would get bare As. It'd be heavy.'

'You're sick tho', bruv, allow burning stuff, you're an . . . wass the word . . . arsonist, bruv.' The taller boy laughed and pushed the other who pulled a lighter from his pocket which he began angling at the air, admiring the flame.

'Yeah I am, I could burn dat bin over there, dis whole patcha grass, da trees, da sports centre, dat girl's butters coat . . . actually that coat *needs* to be burnin' . . . ' the boy said, peering closer at Abigail's Naf-Naf puffa coat.

Abigail slowly carried on biting chunks out of her sandwich and trying to swallow them, wishing her coat would
swallow her up instead. Hide her like a Russian doll.

'Hey, you, yes, you . . . I wrote you a beautiful poem,
shall I recite it?'

The boy flashed a smile and dramatically cleared his
throat . . . I MC you see, so I'll free style for you. Okay, you
ready?

> *Little miss Naf-Naf*
> *sat on her pom pom*
> *eating some bits of shit*
> *along came an arsonist*
> *with a flame and petrol fluid*
> *and fucking burnt the bitch . . . '*

Then he roared with laughter, his little maggots of
cornrows shaking as he did. The friend smiled and tried
not to laugh. 'You're nuts, man, calm down.'

'Nah, wait. I wanna see how this coat burns, bruv. I ain't
never burnt a Naf-Naf coat. I've dun me a Burberry, Adidas,
Nike, Kappa, La Coste . . . which burns brilliantly if I do say
so myself . . . but Naf-Naf, I ain't never burnt a Naf-Naf . . .
speshly not a big old school yellow one like 'dis . . . ' '

The boy came closer and closer; his flame came closer
and closer. Abigail began to panic. She could already smell

her hair barbecuing, and the way it sizzled and curled up, each strand snatching itself away like a child with a slapped wrist. A tear began to slide down her cheek.

'Oi! Low it, man, you're making her upset. Stop it,' the taller of the two said, 'I wanna eat my chips, come on,' he urged, his eyes lighting up at the sight of the flame, letting it slip that even *he* didn't trust this friend, even *he* didn't know how far it would go.

'I wanna blow up Little Miss Naf-Naf . . . ' the arsonist said. 'Don't cry, Little Miss Naf-Naf or your tears will put my flame out.' He had a lisp that rang on all of his S's; it shook Abigail's brain and her eyes re-filled, the tears brimming over.

The girl with the sketchbook got up to walk away, then changed her mind and turned back, refusing to ignore the confrontation.

'Oi . . . what are you doing?' she shouted. 'That's my friend.'

'Agh what? I'm sorry, Jade, I didn't know, man . . . sorry . . . .' The arsonist instantly put his lighter away and pulled himself together, snapped out of it as though he'd been under a spell.

'You will be, you freak. Now find something else to burn. Go on, piss off.' Both boys ran to the canteen door, the taller one lightly slapping the arsonist around the back of his head before they both went inside.

Jade turned to Abigail.

'My mum's best friends with Kieran's mum, the one that tried to burn your coat. If I told my mum about that, she'd tell his mum and he'd be eating his guts for dinner. He's a dick . . . you okay?' Jade asked.

Abigail had never actually spoken to a Goth but she was pretty certain that this was one in front of her, and was grateful to get a better look up close. Jade's face was whitened out and her eyes surrounded by a thick black smudge, one eyebrow was pierced and so was her bottom lip – both with chunky silver hoops. She had a mop of scruffy black hair, a suede coat and boots that would not have looked out of place on Edward Scissor Hands.

Abigail nodded. 'Thank you.'

'K . . . well . . . have a nice day, yeah? And don't let people take the biscuit, you were nearly on fire, remember that . . . '

Abigail hurried inside, unable not to think about Kieran eating his own guts for dinner.

Dear diary

Matt's been fired.... or "asked to leave."

Mum got an answer phone message on the house phone, she rang the College and they said they couldn't give any more details. It's so shit. yeah, ok, he was annoying and a bit of a tryhard but I needed him... even if it was just to shut the boys up. I can't believe that people have so little & to do that they make up such crap...! Can't they be more creative? God, get a hobby.

Something horrible happened today. I don't really want to write about it in case this diary ever gets found... or what if I have kids and I want to show them my old diaries? I don't want them reading about their mum having her coat set on fire! (not that it got set on fire...) It's just... ugh... I feel so paranoid about everything I'm writing now, I would hate to forget all this and then actually <u>believe</u> that those dickheads got away with it and <u>DID</u> manage to set me alight. Maybe I'll start making a new fake life? So when I get older I can read back and pretend that I had a lovely life?

It sounds stupid and cheesy but it's like
Matt always says, maybe i should just
wait until it blows over, that everybody gets bored
and moves on... does something else with their
time... like i dunno... go horse riding or something.
I want to start a new diary and blank the
rest out.

Jade's a goth. It's not a bad look... i'm so
aware of everything i'm writing now... bloody hell!
Jade (the girl that stopped the boy from setting
my coat on fire, who by the way said i was her...
wait for it... FRIEND... F-R-I-E-N-D) is a goth.
There are a few of them but sometimes, they
like to do ~~things~~ things by themselves... like
how Jade was just drawing by herself outside
but then, when she feels like it she can just go
back and hang out with her mates. Easy isn't it?
Rebecca, Florence and Leilah are joined at the hip.
They even all go to the toilet together. They're
so annoying and they hate the Goths... the
goths couldn't care less though... that's what
makes them so cool. I hope Jade talks to
me tomorrow.

I'm thinking about broadening my DVD collection,
dad's got the Charlie Chaplin Collection on boxset.
I think it's quite a good hobby.
I looked on the internet and you DON'T have to be
~~able~~ able to draw to be a fashion
designer! i'm probably going to have to get

~~Would I have to be~~ able to draw to be a fashion designer! I'm probably going to have to get some designs down!

knitted beret... Sienna Miller inspired?

Japanese style hair.

chain mail waistbelt.

'heart-throb logo'

Handle bar anklette

p.s must rember to Copywrite

hoopage... retro? reinforce this with stripes

'heart-throb' logo repeated + bangle

cow girl heel

bootleg flare... perhaps sell to New Look?

defo denim

flower detail hairband inspired by own design... The ring. Clinched in waist.

embroidered detail flower (with extra beads... repeated detail throughout outfit)

Kate Winslet classic, periodic drama inspire "Poofed" look sleeve. Crimped affe

must-have jewel

sequins probably

coral peach tights.

ballet-esque bow-tie anklettes... Clunky heel.

Night ⋆⋆⋆ Abiga...

ACTUALLY..... What the HELL? We all got woken up at 4am... yes 4 am! Why? Because Mum was drilling the wall in, James says. She was just high on Caffeine and had probably run out of Valium.

X Night Abigail

'THE FASHION SHOW' was the line that caught Abigail's eye as she paid for her marshmallow flump at the tuck shop. A bright yellow poster with a picture of Agyness Deyn trying to be all seductive was stuck to the wall. 'Auditions now taking place for Models and Designers.' Abigail couldn't help but drop her jaw a bit. There was nothing she liked more than believing things were fate. It suddenly became clear why she had been thinking about fashion design, perhaps this was destined to happen? She wrote the information on her hand with her gitter gel pen (that had very nearly run out which meant that most of her personal note was written in a white dusty scratch) and felt her body fizzle with excitement and hope. She hadn't seen Jade yet today and wanted to talk to her now more than ever, even just to point the poster out to her. She waited by the tuck shop for twenty-five minutes until she decided to go into the town and buy a DVD and probably some pick 'n' mix. She liked the chewy eggs so much, they had occurred in her dreams more than once.

'Hey, hey!' a voice called after her. 'Hey wait . . . ' Abigail's first instinct was that it was going to be Leilah or Florence, not Rebecca; she knew her voice better than her own mother's. She kept walking, it had happened before where her name had been called and she had turned around only to see a group of people laughing at her.

'Hey . . . !' An arm caught her puffa coat and some of the white puff poured out. It was Jade. She was wearing a worn out 'Siouxsie and the Banshees' t-shirt with a black denim jacket and black leather trousers. She had a heavy clunky silver charm around her neck that perfectly framed her whitened face. 'Oops . . . sorry.' She laughed awkwardly, handing her the bit of loose fluff. 'Hi, didn't you hear me shouting? I want you to meet my friends.' Abigail did not know what to say. She was trying to be nice, even though she was convinced this was a trick.

'Erm. Okay,' she managed to gurgle, and then began walking round the back of the steps, the sunshine on the grass, the leaves dancing on the tarmac. Abigail's bones were rattling in her body, like jangling alarm bells, preparing her body to go into overdrive. Trusting Jade, she followed her to a small brick arch.

'Come on, slow coach. Now watch your head,' she said as she put her own hand on top of Abigail's and led her into the arch.

'Everyone, this is Abigail.'

Sitting in a small semi-circle were a group of about eight Goths, all dressed similarly to Jade. Most of them had piercings and wore black lipstick – even the boys.

'You all right, Abigail?' said one vampire, his arms behind his head, a cigarette perched in the corner of his mouth.

milk toffees.   from

53

'Hi, girl. I love your hair,' spoke another vampire; this one was small and chubby with large boobs. Abigail was shocked when the girl began to stroke her hair. 'Yeah, you're cute.' She continued as though she were answering a question, 'Do you like my fairy wings? I made them myself.' She hummed like a deathly butterfly. So, a moth basically.

'Do you smoke?' Another boy prodded his wrist against her elbow, offering her a cigarette. Abigail shook her head.

'Course she doesn't, Lucas, you tit.' Jade bat the fag out of Lucas's hand and put her hands on her hips, 'You must like cider though?'

Abigail had never been drunk before. It was a very strange feeling, especially at four o'clock in the afternoon. Her brain was tickling itself, tripping over its own thoughts and sentences. She began to daydream. It was as if her brain had been dropped onto an ice rink – like a frozen chicken, and clowns were kicking her brain about, knocking it on the sides of the rink while the audience applauded and cried with laughter.

'What do you think, Abigail? Häagan Dazs or Ben and Jerry's?' Jade asked her.

'Sorry? Jerry who?' Abigail slurred.

'The ice cream, you fruit cake.'

'Oh, I've never tried it. Not properly anyway.'

'PHH, yeah right,' laughed a ginger boy with a piggy nose and a sweaty head.

'No.' Abigail rocked, swaying in her seat, her eyes flapping up and down as though she had penny coins stuck to the lids.

'You're pissed, mate,' grizzled the small busty girl. 'Haha, you're out of your box, Abi.' They all began to laugh. The smell of cider and old man's BO wafted up her nose and began to make her feel sick.

'Don't laugh at me,' Abigail said abruptly, trying to change the subject but everybody laughed harder. 'Stop laughing at me!' she snapped again. Nobody was laughing to be nasty but it became like one of those moments when you're *not* supposed to laugh and no matter how hard you try you just can't stop. It happened to me once in an art lesson but then I stood on a drawing pin and the laughter naturally wrapped itself up.

'Oi, calm down or you'll get us thrown out – it's the only place we can still get in without ID,' Jade said but even she was finding it difficult to hold her smile back because it was funny, seeing Abigail drunk and working herself into a strop. 'Hey, no one's laughing *at* you, you know, we're admiring you,' Jade soothed.

'Whallever,' Abigail slurred. Her red eyes were tearful.

'You're so endearing,' Jade reassured her, and then something quite strange happened. Out of absolutely nowhere, in the oddness of it all, in the old man's pub with the fag burns on the seats and the beer mats with the ladies' boobies on them, in the stuffy corner, Jade slowly lay her head onto Abigail's shoulder and snuggled into her neck. It was in that sugary drunk fugginess, that suddenly everything became serene. It made Abigail feel as though her head was in a sink of water and all she could do was laugh. She laughed so hard it was as though she was in a trance. Tears began to flicker from her happy eyes and her head tipped back to release a child-like shriek. It was a similar feeling being on a diet for years and then pushing your face into a hammock of cream. Within moments the table was in absolute uproar, the laughter was completely infectious and it did seem, on that Friday, that everything was going to be different from now on.

The next morning Abigail woke up but just not in her bed. She pulled the blanket up to almost cover her entire face and analysed the space. It was her living room.

'Had a little night on the razz, did you? You little rebel,' James tutted, 'Dad had to come and get you last night cos you were so pissed.'

Suddenly she felt like climbing straight back into the shell she had spent years trying to break out from.

I GOT DRUNK! AHHHHHH HHHHHHHHHHHHHHHHHHHHHH////
...

I had cider. lots of cider. Not as much as Jade, wow... but lots of cider. At first the taste was weird but then it just slid down my throat. I just feel like... well so happy basically.

Home is a bit rubbish because Dad apparently had to collect me from the pub. James enjoyed telling me... but who cares? I'm 17 years old and it's not like I have College today. Dad hasn't come home yet from the mechanics, he's taken his old motorbike there, to "see if she's got any juice left in her." Jade's got my house number now! I haven't got a mobile. I might buy one instead of DVDs, it might be a better investment.

OH MY GOD! I completely forgot to say: THERE IS A FASHION SHOW! At College, a real one...I'm going to enter my designs... I'm really hoping my potential and talent leaps off the page. I need to buy one of those portfolio things so I look professional. I think mum might have a spare lever arch folder that I can use. probably for the best.

It's 6pm. Dad's back. He looked at me and laughed which means that everythings' okay and then he made me a sweet tea. I made crumpets for us both and we watched the last bit of Goodfellas on TV. Dad told me when to cover my ears.

When mum came back she was pretty normal. I don't think Dad told her about last night, which was good of him. The house phone didn't ring all day, I kind of wanted Jade to phone... but she didn't... maybe I wrote the number down wrong? I went to bed, wondering why machines were always referred to as "she's." Why is that?

Night X Abigail... I'm so glad I've got a lie in tomorrow!! :)

It's Sunday.

I feel a bit crap today. It's raining really badly, James began moaning that he didn't have a playstation 3, "Everybody has got one, and what have I got? A ticket to shitville that's what." I heard him call Rebecca, he was getting all giddy, he awkwardly invited her over but she must have said no, even I couldn't blame her for that, it was really raining. He ended the phone conversation with a "k... well... I'd really like to see you tomorrow." He's disgusting... and Rebecca's even more disgusting. I wish she would stop pretending to fancy James. If she was from a country it would be Vulgaria... because she's so vulgar.

Dad watched snooker all day. Dry. I wonder if there is a limit on a snooker game, do they just play until someone wins or until the scheduled programme finishes? What happens? Do they just push all the other programmes back later and later, so you end up watching Blue Peter at 2 in the morning?

I did some designs today. I'm going to find the girl that's organising the show tomorrow. I'm nervous. I'm going vegetarian. I don't like mushrooms but cucumber's really nice. Night x Abigail x

'Oi, your boyfriend fucked a student, didn't he?' spat Carla's cheese and onion breath, her big moon face peering down filling Abigail's vision. Abigail instantly moved her eyes to the floor.

'He did, he's a paedophile. He was shagging you and then he started raping,' she added, shaking her head, almost unaware of the junk ejaculating from of her massive mouth. Abigail was positive that this was Carla Fork, as in *the* Carla Fork who fellated Gavin Richards behind Halfords, but she didn't ask. Rebecca waltzed over, her hand already diving into Carla's crisp packet.

'Imagine that though?' added Rebecca, as she separated her handful of crisps. 'Not wanting to have sex with your girlfriend that badly, that you're forced to rape somebody to escape . . . now that's just embarrassing . . . ' She left them with a look as if to say *now try and work that baby out*.

'Seriously, she should get some cream for that neck rash. She's starting to look like a cheese grater.' Carla bitched to Abigail. 'Wait for me, Rebecca . . . !'

Girls can be like that though, dispensable.

Mr Stanton stirred his coffee; his coat was too large for his frame.

'Just so that everyone is on the same page I thought it best to keep you up to date. We are interviewing somebody to replace Matthew Gates, it shouldn't take long, it's just a case of somebody ticking the right boxes. In the meantime, if you have any problems or ever feel like you need to speak to anybody, Glennis from the kitchen has kindly offered to be of assistance to you temporarily. That all right?'

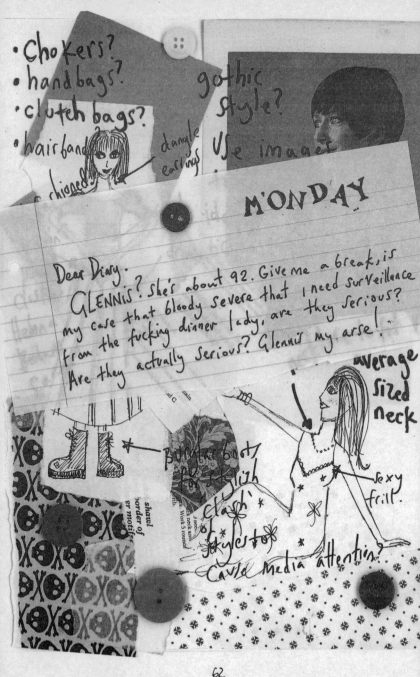

- Chokers?
- handbags?
- clutch bags?
- hairband

gothic Style?
Use images

dangle earrings

MONDAY

Dear Diary.
GLENNIS? She's about 92. Give me a break, is my case that bloody severe that I need surveillance from the fucking dinner lady, are they serious? Are they actually serious? Glennis my arse!.

average sized neck

bovaer boots

clash of styles to

cause media attention?

sexy frill.

shawl border of er motier

62

Abigail walked home with Jade and Lucas. They were arguing over what was better, *Labyrinth* or *E.T.* Abigail and Jade were going with *E.T.* but Lucas disagreed. She left the disagreement at the bus stop.

Abigail opened her front door and, as usual made straight for the stairs when she heard laughter in the kitchen that sounded an awful lot like it was coming from her mum. She stopped at the door to listen, then got the courage to have a peek. There, as large as life, sat Mrs Rodgers with a gown on, a glass of wine in her shiny hands and Rebecca Great giving her 'the chop' that I think was intended to imitate Princess Diana but in fact more echoed that of Gordon Ramsay.

'There you are, my beautiful daughter,' Mrs Rodgers called, holding her wine up to the light. 'Rebecca's training to be a hairdresser, you never told me that.'

Rebecca glanced up at Abigail and offered her a sickly smile.

'I didn't know,' grumbled Abigail.

'Fat lot of good you are, madam. Well, I thought, haircut for free, why the hell not? I took the day off work and everything.' Abigail began to glare at the hair falling to the floor.'Rebecca tells me that you've made friends with some lesbians, that's nice for you, isn't it?' Mrs Rodgers took two tablets and drained her glass.

'You wouldn't be able to give my daughter a quick go around, would you? Her hair is just awful, you see the way it covers her face?'

'I would love to.' Rebecca said, smug as a wedding cake.

'Perfect! I won't have to pay for a haircut again.'

.... The day Rebecca Great cuts my hair is the same day when I eat my own shit. That just isn't happening. Mum's an absolute retard anyway. What the hell? Why is Rebecca even in my house when James isn't even here? And why the hell isn't Mum at work? It just makes it 10 times worse that she's taken the day off to get her ratty locks cut by Rebecca's poxy little fingers.

GRRRRRRRRRRR!!!!....

The door just went. That's probably James ~~saying~~ now... yeah that's him. They're so gross. I think they're a couple now. James is so patronising. I think he's a sexist. It's just really depressing to think he's nearly 21 and still hasn't managed to wangle himself out of that Barbie stage. He's never quite got over Hannah from S club 7, even though his mates fancied that pokey eyed one... I can't remember her name right now.

He's ridiculous anyway, actual women do not ~~like~~ look like that, how many mums do you ~~think~~ see in Somerfields that look like that, or even resemble that kind of person... Zilcho nilcho, that's how many.

Jade's taking me shopping tomorrow. ~~but~~ ~~XXXX~~ I might buy something. I had to peel the potatoes for dinner. I cut the top off my left finger with the potato peeler, and ~~there~~ there was blood everywhere. Nobody even cared that I cut it. Mum said I had butter fingers and was clumsy. She then went on to say, "that's why you're not allowed to use the potato peeler" as if I had been told previously that I wasn't valid to use the peeler. I sprayed some Savlon on it and put a plaster on, the blood didn't stop though. Just now I peeled the plaster off and it really hurts. It looks like a tuna steak, fleshy and pink. My only saving grace is that I don't know where the tip of my finger went. Hopefully it was in the mash somewhere and Rebecca ate it... HA HA! The top of my finger lost in her belly somewhere, swearing at her organs! HA HA! I pretended I felt sick and said I didn't feel like eating, which really pissed me off because I love sausages. Dad came in quietly and put a cheese and pickle sandwich on my desk. I wish he had brought me some crisps too... maybe a drink... I'm well dehydrated.

I spent the rest of the evening in my room.
Mum asked if I was going anorexic. ·
Rebecca looked jealous when she asked me that,
she was probably annoyed that she didn't
have the initiative or the discipline to be an
anorexic. Where as I have that kind of mysterious
aura that gives people that kind of impression.

Who gives a shit anyway?, she sucks my
brother's balls.

'This is the mental Goth shit, like sluts wear this stuff, you see the holes here and here? That's for boobs.' Jade seemed to know her way around Aggressive Angel. She acknowledged the man behind the counter.

'He sells me drugs,' she said dismissively. 'Only joking . . . Gosh, Abi, you're such a prude.'

Abigail put her head to the floor; she didn't want to be a prude. She wanted to be like Jade, confident and striking, intelligent with political views. Abigail's eyes widened at the sight of the chains and shiny leather trousers, the hats and fairy wings, the winding stream of Edward Scissor Hand boots that bordered the walls of the shop.

'Rah! Check these babies out,' Jade yelled across the shop, holding up a pair of chunky boots; but Abigail was in an entirely different place, drifting off into a daydream, her eyes glazing over. She had never seen so much beautiful make-up. The glitters raked up like treasure, sparkling under the fairy lights. The lipsticks and clay pots were filled with face paint and blushers of exotic colours, bright and luminous pastes and creams in tubes and palettes. Abigail wanted to dig her hands into the creams, to spread the textures over her skin and pour the glitter into her hair.

A bald-headed man came over with a full face of theatrical make-up. 'You all right, lurve?' he pouted,

lining up the nail varnishes. This put Abigail off rubbing
herself with the colours and she had to settle for taking a
mental photograph before heading over to find Jade. The
man with the bald head blew her a kiss.

'Do you want a McDonalds?' Jade asked.

'I thought you were vegetarian?' Abigail turned to her in surprise.

'Yeah, but only between 7am and 4pm.' Abigail could deal with that.

As the two of them waited for their orders, Jade lifted herself up onto the counter. The employees looked disapprovingly at her scruffy dark hair, her stripy tights with the holes in the knee.

'Oi, Billy, look, it's the Addams Family,' a boy with brown curtains and a gap in his teeth as big as a bridge shouted from across the restaurant. *Budda ba ba, click click, budda ba ba, click click . . . they're creaky and they're kooky, I pressed your mum in her wooky, she put my dick in her mouth and she choky . . . the Addams family*!!!!' Then he and his friends began laughing and smacking hands like a bunch of hyenas, wiping their souless tears from under dingy eyes, snorting repulsively.

Abigail stared at the floor, focusing on a soggy chip, and wanted to leave. Her body was stiff and motionless. Jade got off the counter and slowly began to stroll over to the boys, clapping her hands, admiring their performance.

'What a wonderful show, boys, you guys should form a band.' She spoke confidently, deep and sarcastic.

'Maybe your mouth and my dick should form a band,' the boy with the curtains croaked.

'Now, that *would* be witchcraft, wouldn't it?' Jade hissed. 'Get some balls and fuck off. Come on, Abigail.' She picked up their paper bags full of food and linked Abigail's arm. Abigail focused on Jade's chipped black nail varnish and then at her own bitten nails, the sore edges, the left over odd strays of loose skin.

'Bye, Lezzas!' yelped another of the boys but the curtain-haired one shut him down with his arm as if to say *that girl's nuts, don't provoke her.*

'I love the gherkins, do you?' Jade smiled, smacking her lips, sucking every finger. 'I usually hate them, but they taste so good on these burgers.'

'I like the . . . erm . . . softness of the bun.' Abigail muttered, trying to think of something insightful to say.

'Yeah, they are soft, aren't they? Fluffy . . . it's like eating the inside of your coat.'

Both girls began to laugh, they swung their heads back and indulged in the laughter, feeling their bellies ripple under their barbecue-stained fingers.

'Do you ever think about killing anybody?' Jade asked, taming the laughter, pulling strings of burger out of her teeth.

'I haven't thought about it.' Which was a lie probably, but we aren't to get involved. 'Why? Have you?'

'Yeah.' Jade swallowed air and focused her eyes on Abigail. 'Myself.' She looked down and slowly pulled up the sleeve of her jumper. Abigail prepared herself for what she was about to see, she thought hard about Jade and how wonderful she was, and how dreadful this was going to be. The sleeve continued to come up until all that was visible were six letters written in black marker. '**HA HA HA**!'

'As if I'd cut myself, Miss Gullible.' Jade playfully shoved Abigail's shoulder. 'You believed me didn't you?'

'I didn't want to believe you, Jade,' Abigail smiled, slightly embarrassed. 'I'm glad it's not true.'

Abigail and Jade split ways at the bus stop where Jade waited for a bus and Abigail turned off to walk home.

'Do you want to come to my house tomorrow after college?' Jade asked.

'Sure.' Her answer warmed Jade with certainty, it was relieving.

'See you tomorrow then, Wifey,' Jade giggled.

'Oh Jade, have you seen the poster for that fashion show?' Abigail asked.

'Yeah. Melissa's organising it.'

'Melissa?'

'You thinking about entering?' Jade asked. Abigail went the colour of a pimple, not a yellow one, a big red one ... I'll start that again. Abigail went the colour of ... a bus? No?

Abigail blushed, that's better, easier at least. Yeah.'

'Good for you, Abi, you better hurry up though, you haven't got long. I'll introduce you to Melissa tomorrow. I used to go to karate with her until she got into fake nails and puppy dogs ... Oh, by the way, that Rebecca Great, that girl in your history class, don't let her give you shit,

Abigail, I've seen the way she looks at you and I don't like it. If she ever says anything to you- you tell me okay? . . . bye, girly!' She waved and turned away.

Abigail's face was hidden under her hair, her mouth tucked down into her puffa jacket, but behind the zip she was beaming. As she bounced her way home she put her hand into her pocket to find her door keys and felt something that she did not recognise. It was a lipstick. She picked at the plastic and removed the wrapper. Then she marvelled at the casing; flicking the lid up and down and admiring the looped writing that read *Aggressive Angel.* She lifted off the, and twisted the base and out popped the shiny black waxy stick, unused and untouched, unlike the hand-me-downs from her mum, which had been shaped by her mother's lips, and which retained flecks of loose flaky skin on the tip. She let herself in, got a glass of milk and some digestives and went upstairs.

Dear diary,

I don't believe i'm saying this... but my lips are black. I have lipstick on right this moment. Black lips! it's weird. It makes my teeth look grey, ghostly almost. My skin is well pale, I think I should invest in a tantowel? That's what the girls at college say anyways, maybe they're right? I look well like a witch. well at least I won't need that white make-up stuff that Jade wears.

I wish mum would walk in. She'd freak! Haha!

I went to Aggressive Angel today. I can't believe I've never noticed it before! It's right on the high street. It's so weird in there they have capes and cloaks and fishnet tights. Jade loves it in there. Jade told me that she has done a few *****, only mushrooms, weed and poppers. They sold poppers in Agressive Angel. Jade said they do exactly what they say on the bottle, cost you £3 to give you a 3 minute high and kill 3 of your brain cells. Sounds stupid to me. She also has smoked *** before, but not regularly like Lucas. Thank Goodness.

75

Aggressive Angel has really inspired me, there is a whole market for Gothic fashion, I could really ~~bla bl~~ stretch myself as a ~~width~~ designer, take a professional curve, maybe I could do a gothic range for Jade and her friends to model for me? It could really work. I'm going to use

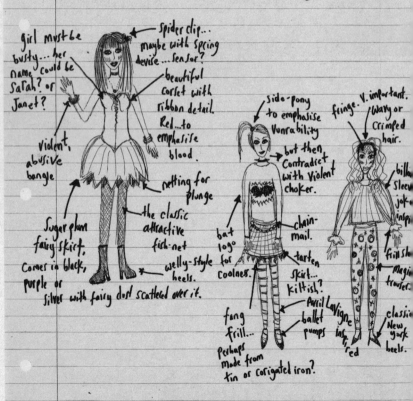

girl must be busty... her name could be Sarah? or Janet?

spider clip... maybe with spring devise... sensor?

beautiful corset with ribbon detail. Red... to emphasise blood.

Side-pony to emphasise vunrability but then, contradict with violent choker.

fringe. V. important. wavy or crimped hair.

Violent, abusive bangle

netting for plunge

the classic attractive fish-net

billowy sleeve joke inspired

Sugar plum fairy skirt. Comes in black, purple or silver with fairy dust scattered over it.

bat logo for coolness.

chain-mail.

tartan skirt... kiltish?

welly-style heels.

frill sleeve magic trousers

fang frill... Perhaps made from tin or corigated iron?

Avril Lavigne ballet pumps

Avril Lavigne inspired red

classic New York heels.

the sewing machines at ~~College~~ College tomorrow,
get some of my designs up on their feet.

Jade got my lipstick from Aggressive
Angel, but I don't know if she paid for it
exactly because I was pretty much at the
till the entire time and I didn't see her pay
for anything. I hope she didn't steal it. Not
because I think that it's wrong. I just can't
picture myself stealing and I don't want to
think of her doing anything that I wouldn't
do. I think Jade could be my best friend.
I hope I'm hers.

Abigail x

Melissa was a complete airhead; Abigail could see that even from their first meeting. It was as though her brain had been removed and replaced with sponge cake. Her skin was beautiful, a golden honeycomb colour and it glowed. She clearly spent a lot of time on her skin, exfoliating and moisturising, and her make-up was no different. Her eyebrows were perfectly shaped and her mascara was clumpless, the lashes effortlessly curled around doughy, soft and shiny eyes. Melissa wore a black vest top that was about 4 sizes too small, although she was short, and she was round-ish, a tad like a pretty, tanned meatball . . . even though she smelt like gingerbread. But Abigail could imagine boys falling for her hard. Everything Melissa wore was designer; Versace, Prada, Louis Vuitton. She had highlights in her straight hair and applied these (hideous) artificial nails that masqueraded as a French manicure and on the tip of each nail perched a diamante.

'All right, babes, have you got any like designs that you could like show us?' Melissa was drinking a Starbucks, the cream leaking out of the sides.

'Yes I have, here they are.' Abigail handed Melissa her scrapbook. Melissa pretended to look as though she knew what she was doing, secretly pleased that people came to her with their designs, that she was the one to decide if they were good enough and that nobody had actually worked out that really, inside her head was a lost pig doing hopscotch. Page by page she looked over the designs, the obscure 80s pieces, and the magazine cutouts from decades ago and then the Gothic section.

'Right, it's quite random, ain't it, babes? Bit edgy? I like it, though it's a bit weird innit?' Melissa smiled, she thought it was funny. Her fake nails tapped the desk. 'We ain't got nothing like this, you made any of this up yet, babes?'

Abigail shook her head.

'You know the catwalk runs Friday, don't you, babes? You got a couple of girls that can help you get it made up?'

'Course she has,' Jade blurted. 'We'll do whatever it takes to get it done.'

'Wicked. Okay, you're in, babes. Last year the fashion show sold out and the winner got her outfit worn by me for the whole day at college. Then we made up these cute little t-shirts with her name on em and went down to the club Squash. You know. Down Camble Road? And handed out flyers and then we got smashed on Sambucca.'

'Great,' Jade snorted, she was clearly irritated by the lost pig of a brain that Melissa had. 'Does the winner get anything good out of it?'

'Well, a load of people enter cos we like get some well good press down to it and like a couple of good designers too, to be confirmed, but still, it's like well good innit?'

'Who won last year?' Jade asked, straightening her voice.

'You know Rebecca Great?'

'Yeah, we know Rebecca,' Jade sighed.

Jade, Abigail and two of Jade's vampires stayed at college until Security asked them to leave. They had put together five pieces from Abigail's collection which now stood proudly on mannequins waiting for Friday.

'All right we're leaving . . . God get a life,' Jade dug at Security as she left.

'They're only doing their job, Jade,' Abigail began.

'I'm only pissing about with them, but just because they're big men doesn't mean they can intimidate us. I won't have their bullshit. Anyway, your designs look fucking mean, Abigail Rodgers. Well done, mate.'

'Thanks. Melissa's funny, isn't she?' Abigail said, trying to change the subject so as not to go bright purple with embarrassment.

'She's harmless, it frustrates me how stupid she is, but what can she do? She fucks bouncers, that's just the kind of girl she is. You hungry?'

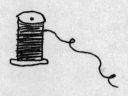

Dear diary.

Today was really, really, REALLY exciting!

First of all Melissa ('babes') said yes to my designs which means i'm in for friday. I've just got a load of work to do before then. Jade and her friends have agreed to model my clothes, which i'm well happy about. Today we stayed in the sewing room till 7.30. We made 5 different pieces. I'm so pleased. Jade has had such a good influence on me. She makes me feel confident and well, I know it sounds cheesy... but kind of cool too.

As for Rebecca great she can rot in hell! I can't believe she won last years fashion show! What is she some sort of maverick? She actually thinks she is good at everything doesn't she? I'm sick of her worming her stupid little way into my life!

She even wrote a creepy weird note to mum and left it on the kitchen table, which I have taken the trouble to put in the paper shredder.

Its supposed to snow tomorrow. I hope it doesn't - i've got loads of work to do before friday.

I think Dragon's Den is my favourite programme.

Abigail xxx

82

Abigail looked at herself in the mirror. Saw her pale thin arms; they were almost blue. Her unbrushed hair sat in a tangle on top of her head. She reached for her lipstick, flipped the lid off, wound up the base and coloured her dry lips in black. Her bedroom was pretty much identical to how it had been decorated when she was nine. She still had a bunk bed but once Mrs Rodgers had realised that no friends would be sleeping over, as in, ever, she had removed the bottom bunk. Abigail now stores her 'stuff' under there; an old tape player with the odd David Bowie tape that her dad had given her. She was never one for music. The rest of her 'stuff' consists of a few books, a couple of soft toys (most of them have scissors stuck in their chests or have been *customised* . . . don't ask) and a small DVD collection. Abigail doesn't need stuff. She has her small TV attached to her wall by a steel frame and that's about it, except for the mountain of empty sweet wrappers that sit next to her bed; sherbet sticks, Malteasers, Skittles, Revels, Minstrels, space dust . . .

Abigail pressed the ON button of her small TV and climbed the ladder to her bed, where she lay down and let the mattress carry her worries for the night.

When she woke up Abigail looked out of the window. No sign of any snow. She put an extra jumper on over her usual dolphin one and reapplied the black lipstick, shrugged on her puffa jacket on and left the house. On the walk to college, her eyes started to water in the cold and Abigail began to feel slightly paranoid about the dark lipstick. Of course, she wasn't wearing it to be beautifull but it seemed to her that the yellow of the coat complemented the black of her lips in a *bumblebee* kind of way and she wasn't comfortable with it. But black can't easily be wiped off; once it's on it's on.

Jade was leaning against the barrier rolling a cigarette. She had no make-up on today and Abigail thought she looked prettier than ever, although not in a lesbian kind of way.

'Hi, Jade,' Abigail said, but this was unheard through the jacket.

'Why have you got your mouth in your coat?'

'I haven't.'

'Yeah you have.'

'No.'

'You've got that lipstick on, haven't you?' Jade smirked playfully.

'Yeah, why? Do I look stupid?' Abigail's eyes widened behind her fringe; she felt clumsy and big, as though she was taking up too much space.

'Well how can I see if your head is rammed in that coat?' Jade lit her cigarette.

'Don't smoke here, you'll get in trouble,' Abigail started.

'Fuck off. Let me see your mouth.'

Abigail slowly unzipped the top of her jacket to reveal her black lips. Jade put her cigarette out on the wall and balanced the remainder of the rollie in the brickwork.

'You look gorgeous, you so look coo'.'

Abigail was extremely shy and began to pretend that the stuffing in her coat was falling out and really needed pushing back in. She shifted her eyes onto the grass. A sparrow edged along the fence, focusing on the crust of a sandwich left on the tarmac. It was so cold; grey smoke leaked from their mouths and nostrils as they breathed.

'How funny is it the day you wear lipstick is the day I go bare? . . . tut tut tut, our stars have crossed, Miss Abigail Rodgers.'

Abigail liked to imagine their stars crossing.

Jade's vampires were under the arches with an iPod, all of them crouched around the headphones.

'Wait, wait for this piano solo . . .'

'It's just exquisite.'

These were the sort of sentences the vampires indulged in. It made Abigail laugh.

'Do you like classical music, Abigail?' one of them, quizzed.

'Do you mean like Christmas music?' Abigail asked. 'I don't like Christmas,' she sighed.

'What the hell? Who doesn't like Christmas?' Lucas screeched. 'Even I like Christmas. I love the food, the music, the presents, the crappy TV.'

'Not much really goes on at my house. My mum sleeps at Christmas, it's just a bit, I dunno, boring.'

'*Boring?*' It was completely antistereotype and difficult to believe, but the vampires did not live up to their name at all, vampires that like classical music and like Christmas.

'And we do yoga!' another added. (Now they are just pushing it, we want it to seem believable so we'll ignore that bit.)

'Come on, you lot, get up off your arses, it's the fashion show tomorrow so we gotta work really hard for Abi.' The vampires begrudgingly got up and stood to attention. Most of them were stoned and could barely stand up straight. Abigail looked concerned.

They headed over to the art department in a snaking black line, which would probably be quite a nice piece of cinematography if this were a film . . . except this isn't a film, is it? This is a book . . . *boring*. The room was full. 'Ugh, sick, the bulimics are here,' Lucas commented, darting his head over to the corner of the room where four pasty, ghost-like figures sat with their bodies hunched over, their spines bulging out of their fishbone backs, their wispy hair in top knots like dishevelled ballet dancers. On the other side of the room Seth and Karl argued over a tape measure, they had Philip on a chair and were wrapping silk around him. To the back of the class a group of Asian girls had a line of models dressed up in saris. Then Rebecca appeared. Florence and Leilah sheepishly scurried after her. She beelined for Abigail. Florence and Leilah nudged each other laughing.

'I heard you're entering the fashion show,' Rebecca snarled

'Don't start, Rebecca,' Jade warned.

'Oh, don't worry. I won't. I just wanted to wish Abigail luck for tomorrow.'

'Bullshit. As if?' Jade hissed.

'No, I do . . . good luck, Abigail. Melissa told me how "quirky" your little designs are; I've heard they're really good for somebody so inexperienced. I'm totally looking forward to seeing them . . . in the flesh.' Rebecca eyed up

Jade, as she walked out of the room . . . . it was a bit like a film again.

'Bitch,' Jade said under her breath.

Once more, Abigail and her new friends worked until Security threw them out. They talked about sausage dogs and their favourite parks and somehow got onto the subject of their grandmas, which again turned into another disagreement between Lucas and Jade: 'Whose granny was more *stylish'*. Abigail bought a Chomp for everybody that had helped her and left with Jade to head back home.

'How you feeling about tomorrow?' Jade asked.

'If I had never entered I would never had known any different so . . . you know . . . I'm okay,' Abigail said.

'Well, Lucas has got a free house tomorrow and his house is sick, so whether you win or not, we're getting wankered afterwards,' Jade said. 'Unless you want to go to Squash with Melissa and snog bouncers.' Jade laughed.

'No, no, that sounds good.'

Abigail got to her front gate and saw a pair of jeans flying out of the top window followed closely by her father's corduroy jacket. The clothes flew out of the window and landed in the hedge.

'JESUS CHRIST, COLIN, LOOK AT THIS SHIT?'

Dear diary...

Mum's throwing Dads stuff out of the window again. She's a nutter. I think her definition of a 'tidy up' is to throw all Dads shit out on the lawn and threaten to divorce him. She obviously has just had a rubbish intense day at work and is being all erratic. She reminds me of that woman from <u>You are what you eat</u>. It bothers me to think some people need to live their life to such a strict regime. I read once that some models eat with a baby knife and fork so they eat less... WEIRDOS! I've seen these girls on a documentry cutting their food up into tiny bite-sized pieces or crunching ice... so twisted... blugh... diets just make the normal people crazy and the crazy crazier.

I'm feeling okay about tomorrow. Nobody has even mentioned it at home. I don't even know if anybody has any idea that I'm talented ... I'm probably a face of the future... in like... design. I'm going to make some toast. James is arguing with mum, he wants a lift to Uni. He says he can't get the bus because the bus smells like piss. Has he never smelt himself? Dick breath.

X

Weaver had his head against the radiator; he had been biting his nails and was slyly pretending to lean his arm over the windowsill to dispose of the bitten ends. At the front of the class Bianca and Jessica held up their map and were telling the class why they had chosen to discuss rock erosion. Marcus had a piece of Sellotape stuck around his index finger and put his hand up to say that he had lost feeling in it and it was going purple. Mr Weaver sent him to the nurse.

'Hi, Mr Weaver, loving your lesson but I've got to go, I'm a main feature at the fashion show this afternoon and we have rehearsals from 3.30.' Rebecca was very good at telling rather than asking and was already halfway to the door; confident she would be allowed to go. Abigail couldn't help but feel slightly annoyed and she could see various other girls in the class looking a bit *ticked off*. Nobody would really say she was a 'main feature' at the fashion show, she was just as important as everybody else. 'Florence and Leilah have to come too, they are my assistants.' Immediately both girls stood to attention, their chairs scraping on the floorboards.

'Okay. Off you go, girls and good luck with the show.'

Abigail was furious. Why was Rebecca lying? There was no rehearsal. What a swine.

Jade was waiting for Abigail when she finished.

'I didn't go to art,' Jade said. 'It's shit. I hate still life.'

'What's still life?' Abigail asked.

'It's like when there are a bunch of pots, jugs and fruit

sitting in the middle of the room and you have to draw it exactly how you see it.'

'That does sound boring. Rebecca's a bitch, she told Mr Weaver she had a rehearsal for the fashion show to get out of class,' Abigail said.

'Who gives a shit. She needs all the extra time she can get. Don't worry about it.'

Outside it began to snow, the white flakes falling like soft feathers. Marcus was out in the snow by himself trying to collect it in a carrier bag.

'Only got two hours to go before the show, you better get your models sorted, Abi. Shall I go and round them up for you? Hey, you should go and photocopy your original designs? You could sell them as prints?'

'Nobody would buy my drawings,' Abigail said.

'I would,' Jade grinned. 'I'll meet you in the studio.'

Abigail suddenly felt a tingling sensation running through her body. I think it was a concoction of excitement and adrenaline. Jade *believed* in her. Jade *believed* in Abigail like a man believed in his beard, like a tot believed in Santa, like I believed if you covered your teeth with coal and slept with it overnight it made your teeth white and found out the hard way . . . Abigail couldn't wait to get started, to get the models dressed up and begin the show. This was the first time in as long as she could remember where she had actually felt excited.

Christina Kerrigan met her at the door to the sewing room, 'Abigail, I don't know what happened. I wasn't here when it happened. I'm sorry . . . ' Christina was one of those girls that was always sick, always going to the hospital, always in bed with the flu, always pregnant.

'When what happened?' Abigail asked.

'Your clothes. They're ruined.'

Abigail ran to her workstation and just as Christina had said, there were her designs in pieces. Drapes of material strewn across the floor, the corsets ripped up and the tights with burn marks through them. The sewing machine she had been working on had chewed up her last piece of work, netting and silk scrambled round the needle. If that wasn't terrible enough, her original drawings had been torn up and some were burnt – all of them were defaced in red marker:

'TRY HARD, UGLY SHY BITCH.'

'UGLY SHY GIRL'S A MIINGER.'

'UGLY SHY GIRL EATS DICK FOR BREAKFAST.'

Christina began to cry. 'I've got a migraine,' she sobbed and threw herself down on her work area. Jade, Lucas and the vampires were coming towards the sewing room; Abigail could hear them chanting the notes of Tchaikovsky's *Swan Lake* as they pounded down the corridor. Jade popped her head round the door, then Lucas followed with a bunch of flowers (they were a bit cheap to be honest, they didn't exactly push the boat out . . . never mind). Abigail burst into tears. Jade quickly spotted the fallen mannequins, the torn material and broken sewing machine.

'Christina! Who DID this?' Jade roared as she picked up the ruined clothes.

'I don't know,' Christina cried.

'Don't lie, Christina. Who did this?'

'I have a migraine.'

'WHO DID IT?'

'Rebecca . . . Rebecca Great,' and her head fell back down into her arms as she cried, 'I have a migraine.'

'Try eating some bloody lunch then, Christina.'

Jade hugged Abigail who had already picked up a needle and thread and was attempting to sew one of the dresses back together.

'That bitch, she's gone way too far now.'

'Oi, Abi, look at me . . . I'm Batman . . . ' Lucas pranced about with some of the torn bits of cloth over his head.

'Lucas, stop being so inappropriate, you twat . . . actually . . . that could work . . . let me see that.'

Melissa climbed her way up the stairs in her silk kitten heels. She wore a white down-to-the-floor see-through dress that made her resemble a fat vase. (Her skin did look good though, I can't tell a lie.) The feedback from the monitors screeched as she went to grasp the microphone. It was very awkward.

'All right, babes . . . I'm Melissa Mannoukas, as you know. Thanks for coming to our second like ever fashion show. We've got some right wicked stuff for you tonight, so enjoy the show and remember to fill out your score boards which you'll find under your seats.'

Shakira blasted out of the speakers and two Spanish-looking girls came strutting down the catwalk in long skirts. One of the girls was at least four moves behind the other, who not only was going far too fast but also had a constipated look upon her face; the audience didn't know whether to clap or not.

Abigail sat in an alcove of the hall; it was fair to say she was 'bricking it' (Jade's phrase).

The bulimics were modelling their own pieces. Their ribs were poking out as they wobbled shakily down the catwalk. Their kneecaps were as large as tennis balls, their shoulderblades forcing out like a set of skis. Some of the boys covered their eyes; the girls couldn't decide if they were jealous or not.

'Stupid 'rexics. I don't get it. I love food. I could never not eat, could you?' Jade whispered.

'No way. Although I think it would be easier to be bulimic than anorexic, at least that way you get to put the food in your mouth,' one of the vampires added.

Melissa took to the stage, this time she was wearing a dress with a barcode on the front reading 'T00 EXPENSIVE 4 U' in black lettering down the side. A top hat sat propped up on her head, coyly slanted to the side.

'How cheap can you get?' Jade murmured.

'Ho no she didn't!' Lucas sniggered.

'I got some wicked designs of my own to show you now, as well as working really hard to get this show up on its feet, plus working towards my B-Tec in dance, I've still managed to squeeze in the time to get my magic from the page, to the stage . . . please welcome Michael, Jack, Hibjul and Ki . . . '

'No fucking way.' Jade's jaw swung open. 'What the . . . ?'

All four boys were greased in oil, dressed only in bow ties and a hideous collection of underwear forced upon them by Melissa. *Could It Be Magic?* by Take That prompted the boys to begin their choreographed dance routine that involved an awful lot of pelvic winds, grinds and thrusts. Melissa found it necessary to do a running commentary.

'Meet Michael, he knows your secrets, see if you can guess his. X sure marks the spot on these bad boys . . . the treasure is yet to be found . . . .' The audience was split into distressed, annoyed or over excited.

'Meet Hibjul . . . the material is from his mother's bridal gown, isn't it beautiful? Kick start your wedding night with a bang by recycling fabrics from your family members, to make that night . . . a *real* night to remember . . . .'

'Is she serious?' Jade shook her head in disbelief.

Once the dry ice had begun to fade and the audience had calmed down . . . and Melissa had changed, yet again, she introduced Abigail's work to the walk.

'All right, babes, I'm like well excited cos now we got summink a bit different. Now at first I weren't sure about this, but Abigail blew me away with her designs. So with pleasure ado will you put your hands together for Abigail Rodgers' first collection . . . like ever . . .'

The majority of the audience was not familiar with the name Abigail Rodgers, so nobody heckled 'Ugly Shy Girl', and nobody laughed at her name or threw mouldy sandwiches onto the catwalk. However the designs were not quite what Abigail had hoped for, thanks to Rebecca, who was being an arse on the other side of the alcove. She had

Florence and Leilah either side of her massaging her shoulders and brushing her hair.

'She's lucky she's all the way over there, I've got a right mind to punch her right in the face . . . ' Jade whispered.

Jade, Lucas and two of the vampires had sewn all of the outfits together to make themselves a cape each and Lucas had downloaded some creepy Rocky Horror Show type organ notes from GarageBand onto a CD and they had simply decided to, well, become vampires. Rebecca shrugged off Leilah and Florence's hands; this was a show she did not want to miss.

Then, one by one the vampires flapped onto the catwalk and began prancing about the stage, spreading their wings and squawking. At first the audience was slightly baffled, unsure how to react, but Jade and her friends were taking it so seriously and doing it with such conviction, it became impossible not to enjoy. A few giggles squeaked out from the back of the hall and it wasn't long before the entire audience was in absolute uproar. I think it became a bit too much when Abigail came down in a harness from the ceiling for the grand finale. The lighting guy, Kevin, was a bit of a geek and certainly enjoyed spiralling the strobe lighting around the room for a 'lightning' effect and, with the help of the sound engineer, Lucy, who had a crush on Kevin, and who was equally eager to impress, had successfully downloaded some thunder snippets from download-asound.com and the two forces together created quite a magical ambience.

The audience wailed with excitement. Even Florence and Leilah were clapping at the side of the catwalk to the beat of the organ. Lucas winked at Leilah who smiled and said, 'This is like so totally random!' as all five of them strutted down the catwalk, making the best of their outfits, their performance and the situation. Abigail was glad to have a mask on, because underneath it her face was a picture of pure absolute happiness and she didn't want to share it with this audience, these kids who had used her, forcing her to want to go home every evening to re-tell her horror stories in her diary, they didn't deserve to see her smile.

Rebecca, however, screamed like a spoilt brat and threw her '*Rebecca Great looks great*' beach ball down. She was dressed in a bikini dotted with hundreds of tiny lips, her spray tan uneven. She marched onto the stage and grabbed the microphone from Melissa, her face fuming.

'They are cheaters . . . !' she screamed. 'That wasn't her original idea. She cheated!'

The audience laughed even harder.

'Stop laughing, you bunch of pricks . . . can you put my music on?' she shouted up to Lucy. 'It's track 7 on the R 'n' B CD . . . ' Lucy mouthed the word 'bitch' to Kevin who laughed. Rebecca prepared herself for her 'sexy beach scene'.

'THAT'S THE WRONG TRACK, YOU FUCKING RETARD!' Rebecca stomped her foot. 'Don't make me come up there and push your face into that fucking CD player, Lucy Dunn, you spastic.'

Melissa took the microphone from Rebecca. 'Listen, babes, that's not cool, okay? Don't be like rude to Lucy, she's like my friend, babes.' The audience booed forcing Rebecca to theatrically flounce off, her long silky hair trailing , her neck rash more vibrant than ever.

'Well, the scores have been counted and it seems that . . . the winner of the fashion show . . . is like . . . my friend Abigail Rodgers!!!! Well done, we're gonna like go down Squash club tonight and wear these well nice t-shirts so if you're free . . . like come down, babes!!'

Abigail took to the stage where she collected her bouquet of flowers, and a crown was placed on her head.

Her friends joined her as the audience rose to give her a standing ovation and Abigail cried and cried with absolute joy.

And it was ... well ... a lovely evening. They all went over to Lucas's house as planned, got very drunk and stayed up till 4am watching *Empire Records*, *The Crow* and dancing to Celine Dion ... and it was probably the end ...

Let me just check that, I'll see if that's how it ended, I have it somewhere here, let me just ... erm ...

I'm just going through the archives now ... fashion show, yep, Rebecca, yep ... blah blah blah ... I've got to get this down, I'm hosting a gathering at 5.

Oh ... oh dear ... no ... no ... that wasn't the ending at all ... let me see how I can end this ...

Right ...

The cape bit, that wasn't a lie, that did actually happen and the audience did quite like it, but let's get real, Abigail was never ever going to win over Rebecca Great, especially not Rebecca Great in a bikini, she really did have a nice set of pins, they looked like glazed baguettes. Rebecca won but it was a very dramatic show all the same. Still Abigail didn't mind; Jade had given the advice to 'rise above it . . . ' she said that Rebecca's fate would be decided for itself. Abigail trusted Jade's philosophy. It seemed to make sense.

Abigail went home before Lucas's party; she had planned to ask her dad if he would get her some beer to take to Lucas's house. However, when she arrived at home, her dad was not there, but instead...Rebecca was, celebrating her success with a glass of champagne, Mrs Rodgers eagerly topping up her glass. Obviously, Abigail was not happy, but she was even LESS happy when Mrs Rodgers suggested that Rebecca give Abigail a haircut. Just as Rebecca was about to begin snipping, Mrs Rodgers received a phone call from James who said that he couldn't get back from university because of the snow, the buses and trains had been cancelled. Mrs Rodgers jumped in the car to collect him, leaving the two girls together. In this time two important things happened. The first was that Rebecca decided to tell Abigail, in a sort of confessions of a serial killer type of way, that she was the one who had stitched up Matthew Gates, branded him a pervert. She cried rape and then went to the college nurse with her sob story so, with that and a used pair of Florence's knickers hidden in his filing cabinet- the story was good to go.

The second thing was that Abigail murdered Rebecca Great, in the bathroom. Smashed her head against the toilet bowl and didn't stop smashing until Rebecca stopped wriggling and her blood mixed in with the blue bubble bath from the broken bottle; pieces of glass floating on the water like tiny sharp boats on a sticky sea. After it happened, Abigail ran out of her house and all the way to town where she sat on the wall of the Cathedral gardens and watched the people go by. The snow continued to fall and had begun to settle, smoothing on the tops of houses, letterboxes, the roofs of cars.

To the best of our knowledge there was only one remaining diary entry found, this was it:

Dear diary, FRIDAY

I've had a lovely day today. It's been snowing but that hasn't stopped us from having plenty of fun - if anything... it's made it better. All my friends and me made a sleigh from an old door that we found in a skip. We took it to the park and took turns in sleighing down the hill. Then we went went to the cinema to watch Back to the future (they were going old school...) I had popcorn and Hagaan Dazs and a bit of Ben and Jerry's to then we walked to pizza Hut and shared a massive pizza! But we didn't pay the ~~bill~~ bill! We ran out without paying, it was so exciting! My mobilephone wouldn't stop ringing like, all day. So many of my friends kept calling and texting me, begging to meet up! Then I got this very unexpected call from the cinema. They said they liked the look of me and asked if I'd be interested in a Saturday job! I kept them waiting for a bit before saying "yes, I suppose I could. Thank you very much." I get £17.99 an hour and I get to let all my friends in and watch whatever film I want - amazing! They have <u>really</u> taken to me.

In the arcade I won £500 on a fruit machine and took everybody to buy make up from Aggressive Angel. I'm in a band now too so I might buy us a rehearsal studio for the day... We're probably going to have a concert too.

Lots of fit boys fancy me too, but I'm in no real rush to get a boyfriend, I just play things by ear, My mum's a film director so I'll probably Move to America and link up with Joshua Jackson and we'll get married and get a sausage dog. I love my life. I'm so happy.

I certainly feel sorry for people that wear yellow puffa jackets and have big ugly fringes with spots on their faces... or Murderers... I feel sorry for them too. I ~~could~~ could never kill anybody. That's just not my style.

Joshua Jackson

engagement ring probably...

Sausage dog

As you can see, even from a first glance, it is dusted with white lies.

Before Abigail met Jade the only tender moment she had ever experienced up to date, was when a bumblebee stung her in the garden. The bumblebee had been hovering over her Coke for a while before she decided to put her hand over the top of the glass to protect her drink from being contaminated by the bee. Not realising that was already in the glass, the bee stung her on the palm. She can still clearly remember lying on her back in agony watching the bee living her regrets. The two of them together, it touched her more than ... well ... everything.

She felt distraught as she scooped the bee up and wrapped her in a leaf before sailing her over the frog-spawned pond. Afterwards she felt fantastic that she had been chosen by the bee for the kiss of death, that the bee had picked Abigail to end her life with, it was a nostalgic feeling, one that she had never forgotten.

Abigail decided to turn back and face the music, she couldn't bear to imagine her father walking in on the scene, the blood, the water, Rebecca face down in the toilet bowl. When Abigail got home, Rebecca's body was missing. No blood on the tiles, no smashed bottle, no flooded toilet. Only Mrs Rodgers reading a newspaper in the living room. Mrs Rodgers welcomed her daughter home and reassured her that she had 'sorted it'. Abigail didn't push the conversation and it was never spoken of again. It is a funny ending, but that's all the information I have.

James came home in tears apologising, he was annoyed that he hadn't put a stop to Rebecca's behaviour earlier. He decided that he was a coward. As time passed he became pretty much dependable in all areas as a brother, Abigail would never feel isolated again as long as he was around. Abigail's father had never been angrier than at this time of his life. As a father I think a situation such as this would make life seem impossible to live. Mr Rodgers outlook on life became hazy and uncomprehending; what used to make sense to him was now utter gibberish. Mr Rodgers got his teeth fixed and decided to train as a driving instructor, he had always been told he would make a good teacher. Abigail was never sure if her father knew what had happened to Rebecca Great and she never asked.

Mrs Rodgers gave up her job; she said she *too* could do with a change of career. She often thought about entering *MasterChef*, she believed she was really rather good at making risotto and it warmed her heart to know that her son had once said that her cooking was 'big in the game'; she assumed that this was a positive response. Mrs Rodgers focused on being a responsible mother; she began by stocking up on Tupperware and investing in a decent iron. Both allowed her to sleep better at night (that and nipping the caffeine in the butt.) The relationship between the Rodgers blossomed like the first signs of spring, gone were the days when they went without speaking, they shared dinner together almost every night, indulging in chilli, ribs, casseroles and shepherds pie, wrapped up warm in the evenings, during one of the longest winters in the history of winters; trying their very best to block out Rebecca Great and her slight case of nappy rash.

It wasn't long before Leila and Florence broke down. Rebecca had been mentally suffocating the girls for years. Rebecca's diary was found two weeks after her death which clearly showed she had had a severe case of depression and self-loathing. Specialists found it to be distressing in places and a shame that she had not sought help before her 'suicide'. The college was damned for their lack of social support for students. Matthew Gates's name was cleared, thank goodness, he soon became a gym fanatic and ate those obscure tablets and drank that strange liquid in order to get that 'ripped' look. Abigail never saw him again. Jade and Abigail went to Amsterdam for a treat. Jade decided she wanted to live there when she was older. James had his 21st birthday party. Abigail DJ'd, snogged two of her brother's friends who then ended up fighting over her and she finished her night off by throwing up at the fire escape; exactly what 18-year-old girls are supposed to do. Which was probably, certainly, for the best.

As the years went by, Abigail wished she could have taken back what she did to Rebecca. Rebecca would have probably grown into a very kind and intelligent woman and had lots of children . . . who could easily have turned into evil bullies themselves, they could have bred like the Gremlins, destroying lots of other people's lives . . . so best not to risk it.

Abigail eventually moved to Amsterdam with Jade and then to New York where she opened her first boutique 'Ugly Shy Girl'. Her first review said that the designs were 'pretentious and overpriced and could only be worn by loony Japanese people' which was true but that's how she got rich.

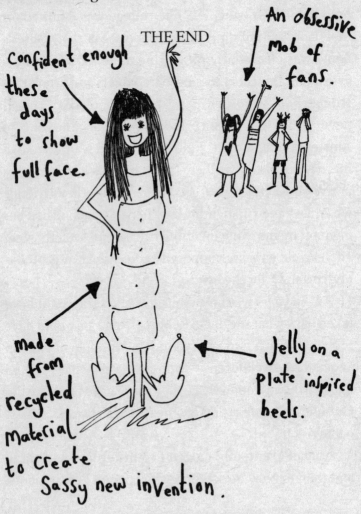

THE END

Confident enough these days to show full face.

An obsessive mob of fans.

made from recycled material to create sassy new invention.

Jelly on a plate inspired heels.

I'll miss you...

Spring Collection

Other people that have made this book:

Claire Bord...
(I know what your'e thinking, looks an awful lot like...)

Kiera Godfrey...

Lee Motley...
always has chewing gum

Terence Caven

Nicole Abel...
always has tea...

Victoria Hughes-Williams

Pat Lomax...

Thank you.